Molly and
the Misfits

Cover illustration by **Roger Payne**

Inside the book. . .

Gavin Rowe illustrated "Molly and the Misfits", "Night Rider" and "For Want of a Saddle".

Valerie Sangster illustrated "The Perfect Pony", **Chris Rothero** illustrated "Out of Sight, Out of Mind" and **Dudley Wynne** illustrated "Cloudburst".

Janet Wickham illustrated "Like a Sack of Potatoes", "A Bit Too Young", "Privileged" and "Not a Novice Ride".

Jane Ettridge illustrated "That's What Friends Are For", "The Expert", "He Just Lay Shuddering" and "Saturday Afternoon".

AWARD PONY STORIES

Molly and the Misfits

...and other pony stories

ROSEMARY SIMMONDS

AWARD PUBLICATIONS

ISBN 0-86163-311-3

Text copyright © 1989 Award Publications Limited

First published 1989
Published by Award Publications Limited,
Spring House, Spring Place
Kentish Town, London NW5 3BH

Printed in the GDR

CONTENTS

For as long as she could remember Molly had helped her father

Molly and the Misfits

Molly Whyte tucked the cuffs of an old pair of rubber-studded gloves under her coat sleeves and pushed thick-socked feet into her wellingtons. A chorus of neighs greeted her when she opened the kitchen door. A twelve-hand Welsh mare named Vixen rapped the stable door with a forefoot demanding breakfast at the double. Molly's boots crunched upon the frosted flagstones as she followed her own clouds of breath across the yard. October had never been so cold!

Vixen had to be fed first or she would sulk for the rest of the day. Molly dropped the other buckets and went in to her warily. The mare bared her teeth and shook her head. She did not bite, which was more than could have been said for her a month ago. Molly patted the mare's chestnut shoulder, ignoring her snarl. "You have improved, you monster," she murmured.

But had she improved enough? The mare had been a menace when she arrived, kicking and biting at the least provocation. Vixen always wanted her own way on rides and reared when she didn't get it. Now, she did not bite often and although her rearing displays were no longer in earnest it would be a long time before she became a safe child's pony. Sadly, Molly turned away with a sigh. If Vixen did not improve quickly, Misty would be sold instead.

Molly put down a bucket for Gentry, a tall young hunter her father was breaking for a friend. Then she came to the tubby bay, Celebrity, due to jump at

Huntleigh that afternoon. Molly did not linger until she was with Misty – Autumn Mist to give him his full title.

The gelding was still scrawny. His bones were easily visible and his coat was like coconut matting. Molly had fallen in love with him at first sight, for no good reason other than he was thin and pathetic and she knew where he would go if they did not buy him. Her father had been against it. They were not a charity, he had told her. An underfed pony, a walking skeleton, cost a fortune to put to rights. Molly had clutched his sleeve, feeling her eyes fill with tears as she thought of what might happen to the pathetic pony nobody wanted.

"Please, Dad!" she pleaded. "I've always wanted a pony of my own, one we won't sell-on to someone else."

"We can't afford to keep a full stable," her father had grumbled. "All the ponies have to pay for themselves." Then, he'd hesitated, watched her eyes and shrugged: "All right, I'll buy him. But if Misty's going to stay you've got to have Vixen sold for me by the end of the month."

That was the problem. How could she get someone to buy Vixen?

For as long as she could remember, Molly had helped her father to run his business as a dealer. Ponies came and ponies went. Molly's special job was to help make sure that difficult ponies were schooled and taught good manners so that they could be sold-on to new owners. "Molly's Misfits," her father

Molly and the Misfits

Molly's special job was to school difficult ponies

called these problem ponies. Vixen had been a misfit all right but even though she was improving, Molly just couldn't imagine her being ready for sale by the end of the month. "It's a real problem!" she sighed out loud.

Molly scratched Misty's shoulder one last time and went back to the house for her own breakfast. The day was busy as show days always are. Gentry and Vixen had to be turned out. Celebrity was brushed until his coat shone and his mane and tail felt like silk. Molly washed his two white feet and padded them with wadding. She bundled him into his travelling gear along with bandages, blankets and their best blue rug. Celebrity was not really a jumping pony, but there would be a lot of people at Huntleigh where he could be shown off at his best in a place where his fine manners would do him credit.

As soon as they arrived and unloaded, Molly stripped Celebrity of his rugs and brushed chequered

quarter-markings over his rump. She saddled him up to ride. Her father wiped mud from her boots with a cloth and handed her a leather-bound whip. "Remember, Molly," he advised, "you don't need to do anything spectacular. Just try to get him round nice and quietly."

"He should be in a showing class," Molly lamented.

"Maybe," agreed her father, "but everyone wants a pony that can jump these days. See what you can do."

Molly walked Celebrity round the perimeter of the parking area to warm him up then found an open space in which to trot a few circles. It was so much harder in the winter. Space was always short and she hated schooling on tarmac. A little after mid-day she noticed her father chatting to a couple and their daughter. The girl's eyes were glued on Celebrity. Smiling, Molly brought the pony back to walk and rode over to them.

"This is Mr. and Mrs. Sigston and Jane," Molly's father told her. "Pop Celebrity over the practice jump for them, would you?"

Molly nodded, looking as if she hadn't a care in the world. She rode to the small practice ring on what had been pasture and was now thawed into mud. As they joined the swarm of

The girl's eyes were glued on Celebrity

small ponies Celebrity pricked his ears and began to think about something other than his next meal. Molly put him into canter three strides out and popped him neatly over the fence.

"Very crafty, Molly. Don't think I missed that," came a voice. Molly looked up in surprise and found Wendy Crew beside her. "What do you mean?" she asked. "Slipping him behind a lead, a real dealers' trick!" said Wendy scornfully. She spun her piebald away before Molly could defend herself with any reply.

A dealers' trick! Molly's lips pressed tight together indignantly. Wait until the jumping – she'd show Wendy she didn't need a lead pony. But her anger soon disappeared. It was impossible to compete against someone like Wendy on her *made* horses. Both girls were about equal in ability but Wendy had skilled mounts and all the time in the world to use them. On the other hand, as soon as a pony became good for Molly it was sold-on and she never had the chance to build up the special relationship needed to forge a winning team. Wendy would always beat her whenever they met – unless she could get Autumn Mist to keep for her very own.

"Molly!" her father called. Molly forced a smile and trotted towards him. "You are next to go," said her father. "Remember, don't hurry him – just go clear. The Sigstons are an ideal family for Celebrity. They want something quiet for the daughter."

Molly nodded and urged Celebrity into a trot. As his feet touched the sawdust he realised he was leaving the other ponies behind. He baulked and Molly had to drive him on with a flurry of heels and a tap from her stick. Molly turned the pony easily into the first jump, driving him on with her seat and her heels. Her concentration was total. The rustic poles, the brush and the parallels were behind them. Celebrity rapped the wall, but from the gasp of the crowd she knew the brick had stayed in place.

Sweat beaded her brow as they cleared the triple bar. They came to the gate too fast, but she didn't dare to check him and it fell. One last fence, a combination, and they were out.

"Four faults!" droned the loudspeaker. Molly patted Celebrity's hot neck. For a pony that had come to them too fat to trot without shivering like a jelly, that had not been bad.

The Sigstons met her in the car park. "He was so calm!" Mrs. Sigston

Celebrity only just cleared the wall!

enthused. Molly caught her father's eye. He winked and she knew that Celebrity had a new home.

"Hi, Molly! I hear you sold Celebrity at the weekend," said Molly's school chum Jenna as she came into Four B's cloakroom. Her schoolbag was already over her shoulder as she buttoned her coat.

"You don't sound pleased. Aren't you going to congratulate me?" chuckled Molly.

Jenna shrugged, then raised a smile. "I was going to buy him myself," she sighed.

"You mean your parents have given way?" asked Molly with excitement, because she knew how long Jenna had been wanting her parents' permission to have her own pony.

"At long last!" cried Jenna. Molly hugged her friend. "Don't you worry, we'll find you something better than him," she promised. "Dad took time off for a sale this afternoon at Biscester. Maybe he'll bring back the perfect

pony for you."

Jenna grinned. "Maybe! Hey, did you hear about Wendy's penfriend?" she added. "She's had her pony stolen." "How awful!" said Molly.

"Aim High is worth a fortune," explained Jenna. "A thousand pounds Wendy said and there's a big reward if anyone finds him. Wendy says he shouldn't be hard to spot. The pony's a brilliant jumper and flicks his tail every time he clears a fence."

"If he ever does clear another fence. You know where stolen ponies go!" Molly reminded her.

"Oh, don't!" shivered Jenna.

"All right, change of subject," laughed Molly. "Tell me about this pony I'm going to find for you."

Jenna grinned and fell into stride: "He's got to be thirteen hands, with a nice face, a quiet temperament and one I won't fall off ..."

Later, Molly and her father were standing in Celebrity's old loose box looking at a classy black pony of around fourteen-two. He had skittish eyes, which he rolled a lot. He swished his tail threateningly, but otherwise he was marvellous. His shoulders were deep and nicely sloping. He had plenty of heart room, clean legs and powerful quarters.

"How did you come by him?" Molly asked.

"Luck!" said her father simply. "Wednesday sales can be a waste of time. You've heard me say that often, but on the other hand you might be able to pick up a bargain. There was hardly anyone to outbid. He's a gift horse, Molly, and you don't ask questions about them." Molly nodded. "He'll have to be kept in over winter," she said.

"That's it – a pony like this one eats money," agreed her father. "Still, he won't be with us long if I'm not mistaken. I'll ride him out tomorrow, see how he goes and you can take him over at the weekend."

The week passed quickly between schoolwork and ponies. Molly rode Vixen for half-an-hour after school, walking, trotting, getting her to stand without fidgeting and to give up her desire to run for home. She was really a brilliant pony, but so moody. Molly came back feeling worn out. Strapping Misty with a wisp to build up his muscles was relaxation by comparison.

The weekend came round. Molly groaned and stretched. It would be so nice to lie in for a change, but Saturday and Sunday were her days to muck out and feed so she forced herself out of bed. She planned her day as she mixed feeds. First it was Vixen she took up onto the moor to give the mare a stretch, coming back through the plantation where they might find something to jump.

They didn't do any schooling today as she was getting bored with it. Molly would not be able to ride Misty for some time yet as his back was too weak. Whether he had been ridden

before they were not sure, though her father thought it likely. So, Molly decided she would try to get a bridle on him. If he accepted it, she would take him for a walk on long reins.

Misty clenched his jaw against the cold snaffle. "What's the matter?" coaxed Molly. "Did you have a hard time last time? Come on, be a good boy for me!" Molly's finger worked into the corner of Misty's mouth and he relented. From then on it was easy, though it took a while to get him walking away from her on the long reins. He had become so used to following her, to knowing she was at his side. Molly talked all the time they walked along the lane, reminding him she was there and, to please her, he walked quietly ahead.

In the afternoon Molly's father led the new pony out of his box and held him while she mounted. "You shouldn't have any trouble with him, Molly," he told his daughter. "He's been fine with me but, just in case, we'll stick to the lanes this afternoon." He checked Molly's stirrups. He tightened the girth from the ground then swung himself into Gentry's saddle to accompany Molly on the ride.

Molly thought it strange to be on a big pony again. She had grown used to riding Vixen and having to lift her feet to clear big jumps. With the new black pony she felt on top of the world. The pony went quietly enough, shying only once when a rabbit ran across their track.

"Do you feel up to jumping him?" asked her father. "Why not, he seems settled enough," smiled Molly. "If that's going to prove he's a no-no we might as well know sooner than later."

The black pony saw the jumps and began to fidget excitedly. Molly bit her lip and tightened her hold, praying he wasn't going to prove a bolter. "In your own time," said her father. Molly nodded, holding the black pony to another figure eight, sitting deep and stretching her heels down to secure herself before she let him go.

He flew the jumps like a bird, his tail whirring. Mr. Whyte put the fences up by two notches and Molly went round again. The pony was steadier this time, springing from his strong quarters and flicking his tail with each success. Mr. Whyte was delighted. "I'll enter you at Cowesby Riding Club Open Day," he told Molly as they rode back. "He'll knock them for six!"

Molly nodded, but she wasn't really listening. Something about the pony's performance niggled at her memory. It was not until she was jumping him alone the following afternoon and heard the swish of his tail with each landing stride that she realised the truth. Molly pulled up sharply, staring at the pony as if he had just sprouted horns. "You can't be!" she breathed. "Not Aim High, the stolen pony!"

Molly rode back, trying hard not to think about it, counting the odds against jumping ponies that flicked their tails. She began to shake. If the pony was Aim High they were now in possession of stolen goods. The police would find out and no-one would believe her father. They never did believe a dealer. Jenna had spoken of a reward but even that would still leave her father's business out of pocket. Her heart almost skipped a beat as she realised her father would have to sell her beloved Misty to make up the money. He was bound to have to do that. There would be no other way.

Days passed and Molly still did not know what to do. They were preparing for the show the following weekend when finally her father tweaked her cheek and said: "You'll knock the smile off Wendy's face, Molly!"

Wendy! There would be no fooling that girl. The blood drained from Molly's cheeks at the thought of Wendy.

"What's up, honey, are you ill?" asked her mother, who generally had very little to do with her husband's stables. Molly shook her head. "It's the new pony. I think he was stolen!" she blurted out.

Molly's mother gasped and sat down quickly. "Go on!" exploded her father in disbelief.

"Wendy's penfriend had a pony stolen three weeks ago, a brilliant show-jumper that flicks his tail when he jumps. If she sees him jumping . . ." Molly tried to explain to her parents. Her father reached out and touched her hands. "It's okay, we'll work something out," he assured her. "What are these people called?"

"Benwell, yes, the girl is Rosalind Benwell. They live somewhere over near Lancaster," said Molly.

"Be careful, Dennis, you don't want them to think you took it," Mrs. Whyte warned her husband. Mr. Whyte smiled at his wife. "It might not even be their pony," he told her. "If it isn't, then maybe they'll buy him to replace the one they have lost!" No-one laughed and Molly went outside to Autumn Mist while her father got in touch with Mr. Benwell.

The Benwells arrived about two o'clock. At the sound of their voices the black pony poked his head over the door and gave a loud whinney. Rosalind ran forward, flinging her arms around his neck, tears pouring

down her cheeks. Mr. Benwell stood back while his wife talked to Mr. Whyte. Molly spied the younger daughter, kicking her feet aimlessly and so decided to make herself useful.

"Would you like to meet the other ponies?" Molly suggested to the young girl, who was called Kendra, and she nodded: "Please!"

At Vixen's door, Kendra Benwell stopped, her eyes opening wide. "She's nice!" said Kendra. "Vixen?" asked Molly in amazement. She was taken aback. She looked again. The blonde girl was rubbing Vixen's forehead and chatting away to the mare. "She's up for sale!" explained Molly.

"Really!" Kendra's eyes were bright. "Does she jump?" "Like a stag," Molly truthfully told her. "Brilliant!" cried Kendra and ran across the yard to tug her mother away.

"Is that mare really for sale?" Mrs. Benwell asked Molly's father, trying to ignore the way her daughter was hanging round Vixen's neck. "Yes!" Mr. Whyte sighed. "She's Molly's old pony. As I was saying, I bought Aim High to replace her and now . . ." Mrs. Benwell nodded. "Could we try her?" she interrupted. "Certainly!" said Mr. Whyte.

Molly tacked Vixen up with trembling

fingers. "You be good!" she whispered to the mare. Molly had no need to worry. Kendra possessed just the right balance of firmness and sympathy to partner with the hot-tempered Vixen perfectly. They cleared a round of tall jumps with ease.

Mrs. Benwell shook her head. "I've spent six months searching for a pony like that!" she enthused. "Name me a price, a good price to include your help with Aim High and I'll pay it!"

So, the deal was done. Molly caught

her father's eye and his wink as she ran back to Misty's stable to fling her arms round her own pony's neck. "You're mine now!" she told him. "Mine!" she laughed delightedly. "Vixen has been sold to good people and no-one will take you away from me now, Misty, not ever!"

The Perfect Pony

When the tangled hedge gave way to white railings, Amanda shifted closer to the car window. In the field nearest the road, four Arab yearlings galloped round under New Zealand rugs, nipping and bucking, full of excitement. It had been enough for her parents to give way to her pleas for an early Christmas present in the shape of something with four legs, but to come to Orchard Stud! Amanda hugged herself. For years she had dreamed of owning an Arab pony.

Her father parked in one corner of the paved yard. Mrs. Pewsey appeared at once. She wore tailored trousers and a white sweater with the sleeves pushed up to reveal tanned forearms. Amanda wished she had put on jodhpurs instead of her jeans, but there was an immovable grass-stain down the left side and this morning tidiness had seemed more important. Her parents had their hands shaken before Mrs. Pewsey turned her attention to Amanda. Mrs. Pewsey's eyes calculated Amanda's weight, height, and the balance of fear and excitement in her eyes.

"I take it you have ridden before?" asked Mrs. Pewsey, her eyes lingering on Amanda's denim jeans,noting also there was no Pony Club tie.

"Amanda was in the school display in aid of Riding for the Disabled," Amanda's mother announced proudly. The display had been one of the things that had clinched Amanda's hopes for a pony – that and a move of house to

"I take it you have ridden before?"

The Garth with its half-acre paddock.

Mrs. Pewsey nodded thoughtfully and smiled: "I've got just the pony!"

She clipped a lead rein to the head-collar of a lightly built fourteen hander and led him into the yard. November sunlight bounced off a burnished copper coat. "This is Fair Wind," said Mrs. Pewsey. He was immaculate – four white socks, an extravagant forelock that covered his eyes and a superbly dished face. "He stands thirteen-three, a bit of an awkward size for us," she admitted. "Too small to show well against the fourteen-two ponies and over the limit for the thirteen-two classes."

Which was why he was at a price Amanda's parents could afford to pay.

Fair Wind pushed his nose forward, snuffing the air with wide-rimmed nostrils. Not quite perfect enough for Mrs. Pewsey, but to Amanda he was pure heaven.

Within a matter of minutes Mrs. Pewsey had saddled the Arab pony

and put him through his smooth paces. Although he was still young he could already show the beautiful floating strides that had entranced Amanda for years. She was in no doubt that Fair Wind would be an absolute knock-out at the shows she would take him to. He was just as wonderful to ride, responding to the lightest touch. As he tucked in his chin to give her a nice square halt Amanda imagined how the show judges would gasp in amazement.

Fair Wind arrived at The Garth the

following weekend and for the next two weeks Amanda existed in a state of bliss. Then the weather changed and those unusually mild days of early December vanished. Now, there was frost on the windows and Fair Wind stood hunched up with his head down low in the corner of the field.

The ground got harder with each day that passed. When Amanda rode Fair Wind out on Saturday morning she had to stick to the roads as the verges were like rutted concrete. Fair Wind kept on shivering and was in a bad temper. "We'll go down to the stream," she told him cheerfully. "A canter will soon warm you up."

As she had hoped, the tracks at the bottom of the woods were still fairly soft. She touched her heels to Fair Wind's sides and clicked her tongue, but he only shook his head and kept walking. "Come on!" Another kick and a tap from the whip and Fair Wind finally dragged his feet into a trot.

When they reached the gate back

onto the road, Fair Wind's head went up, his ears pricking so sharply the tips almost touched. A big roan, built like a tank, came pounding round the corner. Amanda recognized Natalie Jameson as the rider and waved.

"Hello Mandy!" cried Natalie. "So, this is the famous Arab. Very nice!"

Amanda's cheeks pinked. "Thanks!" she said, and added: "Samson is looking in good form." So he did. She had got into a habit of thinking of Samson as a rather lumpish horse, but right now, clipped out and with muscles on his back legs that would make a prize-fighter envious, he looked very impressive.

Natalie rode back to The Garth with Amanda, which pleased her because the company made Fair Wind pep up and he was more like his old self again. "I've just had a thought!" Natalie exclaimed as they entered the yard. "Ferndale Meet is at Langley Green on Saturday. We could go along together!"

"Surely Fair Wind is too young for hunting," Amanda told her. "For a full day, yes," explained Natalie, "but we could go for an hour or so just to give them a run. Don't worry, I'll keep Samson back with you. Tell you what, I'll bring my clippers round this afternoon and give Fair Wind a trace so he won't get too hot."

"Thanks, Natalie . . ." Amanda stopped and felt her cheeks redden as she remembered her pony's hunched appearance that morning. She forced a laugh and said: "Second thoughts, I'd

The Perfect Pony

Fair Wind was more like his old self!

better not. He needs every hair he's got in this weather!"

"You do have a stable for him, don't you?" Natalie's voice was tight. The words hit Amanda like a blow in the stomach and it was a struggle to make her lips smile. "Not yet – I was going to convert one of the sheds this weekend!"

Natalie didn't say anything else. She just looked at Fair Wind, with his tail clamped down, and turned away.

Five minutes later Amanda was in the lounge pleading with her Dad to move his gardening gear into the garage. "And where am I going to put the car if I do that, Mandy?" he asked. "Oh, there'll be room," insisted Amanda. "I'll move the stuff myself. Please, Dad I must have somewhere to bring Fair Wind in at night. It's too cold for him outside."

Her father put down his paper. "You knew we didn't have a proper stable, Amanda," he sighed. "You should have thought about that at the start. Your Mum and I don't know what

different breeds need. We were relying on you."

"I'm sorry, I thought grass would be enough," Amanda pleaded. "Look, if I tidy it all up really well can I give it a try by using the shed?"

With a few more grumbles and complaints her father gave way. Amanda spent the afternoon shifting spades and sacks and towers of plastic plant pots. She then washed out the shed and laid a good bed of straw from a bale which she sweet-talked out of

Mr. Rees up the lane at Garth Farm. The finished article was hardly luxury, but at least it would keep her pony out of the wind.

Then came the last week of school which made the thought of being able to ride in at night because of bad weather just about bearable. On Thursday it started to snow and fat white flakes floated down softly to cover the ground within minutes. As both her parents worked, Amanda decided to keep Fair Wind in the stable for the day. Amanda began to fear he would get pneumonia. On Friday the weather was no better, but Amanda scarcely noticed for counting down the hours until the end of term and freedom from school.

Her father brought a Christmas tree home and they spent the evening adding decorations. Amanda's mother put aside a length of tinsel and some holly to decorate Fair Wind's stable door.

Thankfully, the sky cleared on

Saturday and Amanda was able to ride. Fair Wind was in hight spirits and jumping out of his skin to be outside. He skipped about on the flagstones while she saddled him and was trotting out of the yard before Amanda had sat down in the saddle.

"Now then, steady on," Amanda told him firmly as she drew back the reins. Normally, Fair Wind settled at once. Today, he was having none of it and gave an enormous buck before jogging down the road, his quarters swinging

off the verge. "Stop it!" Amanda scolded and hauled back.

Fair Wind went hard underneath her and for the first time she felt frightened of his strength. Some deep instinct warned that the minute he got hold of the bit there'd be no stopping him.

They managed for a while, pulling at one another but neither winning. Soon they reached a stretch where Amanda usually cantered. Fair Wind began bouncing about and shaking his head. "No!" Amanda insisted. "Walk!" She yanked at the reins.

The next thing she knew she was face down in a snow drift with briars wrapped round one arm and listening to the sound of iron shoes ringing on salted tarmac.

Tears flooded Amanda's eyes as she floundered in pursuit of her pony. The main road was only a mile away.

"Amanda! It's all right!" Natalie's voice called a loud reassurance "I've got him!" Natalie came round the corner leading Fair Wind at Samson's

side. Amanda explained what had happened as they rode back.

"I don't suppose you'll want to hear this," Natalie warned, "but I think you should sell Fair Wind. Honestly, there isn't room to keep him properly at The Garth."

"Never!" Amanda shook her head.

Natalie shrugged. "It is your choice, of course . . ."

Those words kept coming back into Amanda's mind and with them a vision of Samson in the yard. Even she had been forced to admit that the shed looked more like a cupboard than a stable with Samson beside it. Fair Wind had not been pleasant to ride that morning and was a threat to himself. With the worst of the winter yet to come he would become plain dangerous. Amanda struggled on for another two days, telling herself that it would work out, turning Fair Wind out to settle him.

After the fall she was too scared to ride and every time she put him into the shed for the night she was full of guilt. Eventually she came round to the truth that maybe she had been over-enthusiastic in buying Fair Wind.

Full of ideas but not much common sense, she hadn't really known what was involved in owning a horse. Putting her pride behind her, Amanda spoke to her parents.

Fair Wind was sold two days later. Amanda cried, but forced herself to go through with it knowing he'd have gone berserk locked up in her tiny

After the fall she was too scared to ride

stable through the heavy snow of mid-winter.

On Christmas Eve, hoofbeats in the yard made Amanda drop the mince-meat spoon and run to the kitchen window with a fleeting fantasy that Fair Wind had come back. Natalie pulled a small bay mare with a woolly coat and thick curly mane to a halt and dismounted. "I heard about Fair Wind," she told Amanda. "I think you did the right thing." Amanda nodded, her throat too tight to speak. The mare found the sweetness on her fingers and began to lick them.

"What do you think of Bracken?" asked Natalie. "She's not mine. I'm exercising her for someone else. She's up for sale, actually." Her eyes glittered mischievously.

Sale! Amanda's heart leapt into her mouth. Stubbornly she forced the excitement down. She must not make the same mistake again. Bracken did not have the fine points of Fair Wind, but she was a pretty pony just the same. Her eyes showed native spirit. Her features were delicate, yet she was hardy with it and experienced enough to put up with a first-time buyer.

Natalie pulled off her gloves. "Why don't I have word with your Mum while you two get acquainted," she grinned.

For the first time ever, Christmas Morning did not begin with Amanda running to the tree for presents but straight outside to the stable where Bracken was whickering for her breakfast. Amanda fed her mince pies, which she adored before her pony nuts, and stroked the soft coat whilst she ate. There would be time for Arabs later, but right now Amanda knew that the perfect pony for her was right here.

Like a Sack
of Potatoes

If Judy hadn't gone pony trekking last summer none of this story would have happened. Judy came back full of tales about cantering over the heather and the excitement of the gymkhana. Her friend Carolyn listened and the idea of hiring ponies for an afternoon ride became very inviting.

Carolyn was secretly glad when Judy chose Forest Holme Stables. The memory of riding round Hazeldene School, where she had been the only twelve-year-old in a class of much younger infants, was not a pleasant one. It had put her off riding lessons for the rest of her life.

All the way to Forest Holme she tried to imagine what it would be like to ride again, and as she entered the yard her heart beat fast. Judy was standing with Mr. Ford, looking very pretty and complimenting him on his establishment. Not that Carolyn could see much to flatter in the dilapidated yard but Judy, she knew, was trying for a discount on the fee they would have to pay.

"And this is Carolyn," said Judy introducing her friend with a beaming smile. Mr. Ford looked Carolyn up and down, took in the long plaits, anorak and wellingtons and then asked: "You have ridden before, I take it?"

Judy answered for her, plunging into a fantastic account of how they had ridden together on her 'darling' pony, Sophie, who had sadly been sold as her mother was allergic to horses. She sighed and wiped an imaginary tear

Like a Sack of Potatoes

"And this is Carolyn," said Judy

from her eye. Carolyn's jaw dropped. Judy was lying through her teeth. Sophie was her mother's name.

Mr. Ford seemed really touched by the story and Judy, with fair hair falling softly over the turned up collar of her quilted jacket, looked the picture of the distressed damsel. He patted her arm gently. "Don't worry, dear. You'll be welcome to ride here," he assured Judy in a kindly voice.

"Why did you say we could ride?" Carolyn hissed as soon as Mr. Ford was out of sight. She had not been on a horse for nearly two years. "You might not mind an old donkey," said Judy, "but *I* want a horse with a bit of blood."

Hooves clomped on concrete. Fear surged in Carolyn's stomach and her hands clenched so hard that the nails dug into her palms. Judy's smile had vanished. Gritting her teeth, Carolyn turned round, saw the ponies and let out a faint sigh of relief. "Lovely pair, these two," said Mr. Ford. He handed the reins of stocky, thirteen-two Blackie

to Judy. Carolyn's own mount was a very ordinary looking bay mare, Dora.

Reaching for a titbit in her pocket, Carolyn patted Dora's nose. Her confidence was ebbing fast now they were actually close to the beasts. Lop-eared Dora guzzled the sugar lumps, nipped Carolyn's pocket for more then sighed and hopefully eyed the grass verge.

Dora's reins were stiff and toothmarked where she had chewed them. The buckles were rusted. The saddle was worse. Grey stuffing sprouted from the nearside panel and a fat band of sticky tape held together the split leather of the cantle. Carolyn exchanged a look of despair with Judy, who was trying to stop Blackie nipping her as she mounted. Then Carolyn gathered up Dora's reins, turned the stirrup and heaved herself into the saddle.

To Carolyn's surprise they managed to get out of the yard, up the lane and through the forestry gate without mishap. Settling into Dora's placid motion Carolyn found she was almost enjoying herself.

Then Judy decided it was time to trot and fear rose again like a hard lump in Carolyn's throat. She had never been able to get the rhythm right for trotting. Dora, however, had no intention of going faster than walk. Neither would Judy's flapping legs and muttered curses make Blackie speed up.

Elbows turning out like wings, Judy hauled Blackie to a stop and slid off. Her face was crimson. "I've had enough of this!" she snapped, thrusting her

reins into Carolyn's hands. "Lazy swine, I'll teach him to wake up!" Her hands shot out to box Blackie's ears and then she was striding away. Dora stretched her neck to nibble grass and Blackie leaned against her, crushing Carolyn's leg and bringing tears to her eyes.

Judy was shouting that she hadn't paid her money to be lumped about like a sack of potatoes. That, unfortunately, was about all that Carolyn herself felt capable of doing – being lumped around like a sack of potatoes.

Judy returned brandishing two hazel switches. She pressed one into Carolyn's hand. Blackie, suddenly very much awake, set off at a spanking trot. Dora was anxious not to get left behind and followed her stablemate.

Judy used the hazel switch for a whip and brought it down at the least excuse. Carolyn just clung on behind on Dora and wished they were safely back at home. The ponies obviously felt the same, for when the girls finally turned, they seemed to decide to get home as quickly as possible. Almost catching Judy unawares, Blackie got off to a good start. Dora raced alongside, nose in the air. Judy cried out, gathered up looped reins and leaned back with her feet sticking forwards at an outrageous angle as she heaved with all her might. Dora, now completely out of control, flew past. Carolyn got a fleeting glimpse of Judy shouting advice, her blue eyes wide in an ashen face full of fear.

She gathered up looped reins and leaned back

Dora slithered round a corner and Carolyn slipped across the saddle, losing her stirrups. Then there were people ahead. A dog barked excitedly. Dora's ears went back. Someone screamed. Dora swerved. The ground rushed upwards. Stars exploded in Carolyn's head and everything went black around her.

Voices broke through the mist. Carolyn's head throbbed and the faces blurred when she tried to focus on them. "Take it slowly, love," a woman's voice said as Carolyn slipped back into the darkness. The voices came back. "There's nothing broken," someone said. Again, Carolyn struggled to open her eyes. There was a tree, clear against a blue sky. Worried faces hovered beside her.

"Your friend has gone after the pony," the woman said.

Carolyn thanked the family, who had been out walking, and assured them she was all right. She got to her feet and followed the path downhill in an unsteady search for Judy and the ponies.

Round the next bend Judy appeared, leading Dora. She was jubilant. The mare had been caught easily. Carolyn took the reins, looked at the saddle and felt her knees turn to water. Shaking and cold with nervous sweat, she told Judy to ride on ahead while she would lead Dora home. In her heart she knew it would be a long time, if ever, before she would trust herself to ride again.

A Bit
Too Young

"He's yours," Pamela Bowker's father was saying, but she hardly heard him. Every Christmas for the last three years she had asked for a pony and now her dreams had come true. She would be able to ride alongside girls like Ellen Pennyman, compete at gymkhanas and perhaps even win a rosette. In her imagination Pamela executed a perfect flying change and smiled graciously at the judge as she bowed to take the Challenge Cup.

Ridiculous really, since she wasn't even certain exactly what a flying change was. Also, her pony was not in quite the same league as Ellen Pennyman's. He stood about twelve hands high, a strawberry roan with small hooves, a spriggy mane and short curly tail.

"He's been broken in, Pamela, so you'll be able to ride him straight away," her mother said proudly. Frankly she had doubts about buying a pony and worried that maybe young ones were supposed to be on the wild side for youngsters to handle.

"Pretty little thing, just turned two this summer," Mr. Bowker added brightly. "You'll be able to grow alongside each other. Young pony like that will do for life."

Pamela nodded. This was not the time to tell her father that ponies did not just keep on growing. A twelve hands, sort-of-Welsh, would never make a lady's hack. But right now she did not care. She would never have to scrimp and save for riding lessons again.

"What are you going to call him, Pam?" asked Mr. Bowker. She shrugged, thinking first of a stylish name like Strawberry Fayre or Paperchase. Somehow, the only one to stick was Pinky, so 'Pinky' he became.

The Bowkers' back garden was quite big for a semi-detached house and it was agreed that this should become Pinky's field. A second-hand bridle had been thrown in as part of the deal. It was rough but usable and after combined efforts with a pair of nail clippers, two dusters and a tin of Cherry Blossom it soon looked smart enough to use.

The first time Pamela rode Pinky she was full of nerves. She'd had a few lessons and ridden every beach pony she had seen, but this was different.

Fortunately Pinky was good natured and put up with the whole palaver pretty well – he even stood quite still while Pamela checked her bridling

The second-hand bridle was usable

against the picture on a horsy postcard. Once on the drive, however, he began to get excited. Pamela's heart sank, but she did not dare show her fear in case her mother saw and decided he was dangerous and must be sold as soon as possible.

Pinky sprang forward the minute Pamela left the ground. She hung on grimly and two fly-bucks later they were jogging down the road. Pinky had his nose in the air and back uncomfortably hollowed, but at least Pamela was riding him.

By the time they got back, Pamela was aching in every limb. Pinky had shied at every parked car, drain and bicycle. He'd stopped dead where white lines crossed the road and shot across somebody's lawn when a bus came up behind them.

It was going to take a lot of hard slog to put Pinky straight, but Pamela was not about to be beaten.

She rode every day, half-an-hour after school and two hours at weekends.

Within a month Pinky was plodding quietly along the roads and only goggling at buses instead of taking off.

But as one problem was put right, another one grew. Bare patches were replacing the grass in Pinky's field, but before Pamela spent her savings on hay there was a saddle to buy. A good leather one was out of the question, but Pamela had seen an old donkey pad at the saddlers and in a few weeks she had enough money to buy it.

By February even Pamela had to

admit the hay situation was getting bad. Pinky's bony spine made riding him torture and she was glad of his winter coat to cover a shameful display of ribs. Pamela had given up riding on weekdays, but she still took Pinky out at weekends. She let him graze the verges, which he did with the ferocity of a vacuum cleaner. Meanwhile, Pamela sat on his back practising riding exercises.

One morning, halfway through 'Round-the-World', Pamela heard hoofbeats. She had just managed to wriggle back to facing front when Ellen Pennyman, riding an immaculate and blanket-clipped Sergeant Major appeared round the corner.

Pamela struggled to raise a smile. She had boasted at school about having a pony, but as yet no one had seen him. Faced with glossy Sergeant Major, whose thoroughbred blood showed in every vein, Pinky looked positively tatty. Ellen's eyes widened and even Sergeant Major managed an expression of maternal concern, which was quite something for a gelding!

"Hello, Pamela," Ellen began. "Is this Pinky?" Pamela nodded. "How long have you been riding him?" was the next question. "A month," Pamela replied, sensing disapproval.

"He looks a little young," exclaimed Ellen. "He's been broken!" Pamela answered defensively. "But he can't be three yet, Pamela," insisted Ellen. "He really is a bit too young to be ridden, you know."

"He likes going out," snapped Pamela.

"He'll spoil if you ride him now," advised Ellen. "Why don't you turn him out for the winter and start up with him again in May? It would give him a chance to fill out."

By May Pamela had hoped to be jumping. Pinky dragged at her hands as he pulled for grass. Face to face with Ellen, Pamela began to have her first serious doubts. Pinky was young, but he had been broken when she got him and he'd never objected to being ridden.

"He could run with Major over the winter," suggested Ellen.

"I couldn't afford the grazing," Pamela mumbled, wondering as her dreams crumbled how she could ever have really thought the back garden would have been big enough.

"You don't need to pay," continued Ellen. "He's not going to eat me out and Major could do with the company."

"If you are sure it's all right,"

Pamela replied, swallowing her pride. Guilty tears pricked at the back of her eyes as Pinky nibbled her boot. She saw then what having her own pony really meant. His life was in her hands. It was up to her to ensure it was a happy one.

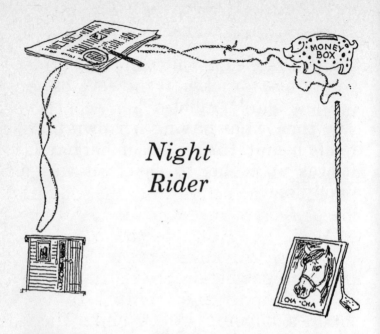

Night
Rider

Whenever Marie looked out of her bedroom window and imagined the coalshed converted into a loosebox, she always saw the same golden head poking over the half-door – Julia Westmond's pony, Cha-Cha. She was a thirteen-hand dun mare with dark eyes and such a kind temperament that even when she shied she seemed to apologise to Julia afterwards.

Marie had given up asking her parents for a pony. They always said 'no' in a very positive manner.

Julia Westmond was two years older than Marie. She would be fifteen this autumn and that meant Cha-Cha would probably go up for sale. Marie had given up riding lessons for the sole purpose of saving up for a pony and her heart was set on Cha-Cha. So far, she had saved up forty pounds.

"Marie!" came her mother's call.

With a sigh, Marie left her thoughts and went downstairs. Her mother was frying onions and pointed to the potatoes bobbing in the sink. There was an open newspaper on the draining board ready for the peelings. That was where she saw the advert for Cha-Cha.

"You're very quiet" said her mother. "It's Cha-Cha, Julia Westmond's pony," said Marie and tears pricked the back of her eyes as she pointed to the paper. Seeing the pleading look and the tears welling, Mrs. Brady put down her spoon and came closer. "How much is it?" she asked. "Three hundred pounds," Marie croaked, then added quickly: 'I've got forty pounds saved towards her."

Mrs. Brady's eyes widened and her cheeks went pink. "Three hundred pounds for a little thing like that!" she exlaimed. "She's well behaved," Marie told her, defending Cha-Cha immediately. Her mother shook her head. "I'm sorry, love, but it's out of the question."

"I know it's a lot, Mum," Marie persisted, "but I'd pay you back, honestly, with a little each week."

"And whose money is going to feed her in the meantime?" asked Mrs. Brady.

She was right – Cha-Cha could not live on thin air. Besides, she was used to good pasture and daily feeds. Marie tried, but could not forgive her mother for saying 'no', nor Julia Westmond for selling Cha-Cha so soon. If only she had waited until the next spring, when her savings would have been so much more. Marie sighed. What did that matter now? It was too late!

That evening, Marie was not able to

If only Cha-Cha didn't cost so much!

concentrate on her homework or bear the thought of watching television with the family, so she went for a walk. Her feet took her from habit to Cha-Cha's field. The dun mare recognised Marie's voice and came trotting over to snuffle her pockets for food.

Where would Cha-Cha go? Would she ever find a pony to replace her? It wasn't fair. She would never even get a chance to ride her now, unless ...

The full moon climbed higher, casting a ghostly shadow into the field. Marie could see very clearly by the silvery light. Her left hand closed around the twist of string in her pocket and suddenly her mind was made up. She climbed over the gate and fastened the makeshift rein to the headcollar Cha-Cha always wore.

Marie's heart was hammering as fear and excitement took hold of her. "Steady old girl!" she whispered to Cha-Cha and took the string in one hand as she vaulted onto the warm back. Cha-Cha tossed her head in

The full moon cast a ghostly shadow over them

surprise but cocked an ear at the sound of Marie's voice and quickly settled to walk around the field for her.

It was wonderful to be riding again. Marie's confidence grew with each stride and before long she tapped the mare's sides for a trot.

Without stirrups or a saddle, the stride was bouncy and she was flung forward and forced to dig her knees into Cha-Cha's sides to stay on. The mare threw up her head with a snort and by the time they had crossed the field Marie had compeltely lost control.

When Cha-Cha tripped in the tussocky grass Marie shrieked, the mare shied and the next thing Marie knew she was sitting in the dirt while Cha-Cha galloped round the field with the string reins trailing dangerously near her forefeet.

"Cha-Cha!" Marie cried desperately. The mare ignored her. She stopped but set off again each time Marie tried to catch her. Tears poured down Marie's cheeks, but there was nothing she could do. Her efforts only made the mare behave more badly.

Marie didn't know if she should go home or go and tell Julia. She was scared to admit what she had done. She

would become and outcast at school and in the village, but she was frightened for Cha-Cha too. Picturing the mare somersaulting with a foot through her reins, Marie ran all the way to Julia's home.

Julia answered the door.

"It's Cha-Cha!" Marie blurted. "The string on her halter ... she'll fall – I

couldn't catch her ... she's too scared!"
Julia did not think to ask Marie what
she was doing up Tidkin Lane at ten
o'clock at night. Her concern was all
for her pony. When they arrived at the
field, Cha-Cha was still on her feet and
let out a plaintive whinney at the
sound of Julia's voice.

"Poor Cha-Cha," said Julia sooth-
ingly as she caught hold of the
headcollar and untied the string. Marie
stepped closer to stroke the mare's
neck. It was matted with sweat. Cha-
Cha jumped aside and rolled an eye at
her.

Julia apologised at once. "It's not
you, Marie," explained Julia. "She was
galloped round this field for an hour by
some kids last summer. We never found
out who did it but they left her in a
dreadful state. She hasn't forgotten it."
A blush scorched Marie's cheeks as she
said: "But she's normally so quiet."

"Only recently," Julia told her. "It
took an age to get her over that last
trouble. At least she doesn't seem so

bad this time. Maybe they were bucked off. That would serve them right, wouldn't it!"

Marie managed to smile, but she felt full of guilt. She had been so concerned with her own problems it had never crossed her mind she could cause just as many herself. Much as she would miss Cha-Cha, she had to admit that the pony might be happier in some other place safer than the field in Tidkin Lane.

Out of Sight, Out of Mind

Chequer wandered across the small paddock with her grey nose only an inch above grass level. Her tail flicked at dozy flies. Queenie ran a circle, stopped and butted her mother's belly, pretending an attempt to suckle. The first time, Chequer thrust at the youngster with bared teeth. The second time, she chased her off and Queenie pelted round the paddock with a squeal of delight.

It would be hard to think of the paddock empty - no whinnies to greet

Queenie pelted round the paddock

me in the morning, no pony running along the side of the fence and bucking when I got home from school. To think all this had to come about because I had wanted to keep Chequer for myself, because I thought I couldn't bear to part with her!

The dapple mare had been everything I could wish for. She was my first pony and it was with her that I won my first rosette. One marvellous day, she and I swept the board at a local show and came home with the challenge cup.

Then came the winter and I was faced with the problem of outgrowing her. Rather than sell her I decided to breed a foal of my own. Dad wasn't too keen. One horse was enough, he said. But Mum rather fancied the idea and I soon convinced her that a foal would be a sweet thing to have.

What a thrilling time that was, leafing through the stallion files. Chequer was New Forest through and through. I had my heart set on putting her to an Arab stallion but there were

none standing close enough so I settled for Timitoo, a thoroughbred. She took first time. With growing excitement we watched her sides fill out, laying odds on whether the foal would be grey, like her mother, or brown. Queenie finally turned out to be just like her mother born in complete privacy before dawn two weeks ahead of time.

Everything should have been fine. The birth had been easy. Queenie was a strong foal and already quite tall. The trouble was that she ate and ate.

89

She packed away the concentrates faster than I could buy them.

"You'll have to ask your Dad," said Mum when I approached her about a rise in pocket money to help me out. Dad shook his head. "You wanted two, so you've got to face up to the responsibility. After all, you are old enough to get a job, Susan."

I spent the next Saturday going round town asking in all the shops for a chance of some weekend work. Luckily, the greengrocer agreed to take me on. The job didn't pay much for the hours I was working, but it was enough to ease the strain of feeding Queenie.

What with working at the shop and revising for exams, I found myself with hardly any time to myself. I missed my rides too. In the past, Chequer and I had enjoyed such fun together.

April 1st! Looking back it certainly was a Fool's Day for me, but of course it didn't seem like that then. I thought that at eight weeks Queenie would be old enough to stand being alone for a bit. Besides, I was desperate to ride Chequer again. "I'm just going out for half-an-hour," I announced as I washed up my breakfast crocks. "It's time they got used to being separated."

"But Queenie's still only a baby!" Mum protested. My cheeks flushed. "No she's not," I argued. "Horses age much faster than humans. If they were on a proper stud they'd be in separate yards by now – out of sight, out of mind."

Mum looked doubtful. Dad was

unusually silent about the whole thing.

I had a bit of a flap on to get Chequer out of the stable without Queenie breaking free, but eventually I managed it. The din was terrific as the two of them started their non-stop neighing. Chequer danced about with her head in the air, bugling as I tried to get on. "Stand still!" I shouted at her. She took no notice. Nerves made me tremble. It seemed so long since I had ridden, but in the end anger got the better of me. I only wanted Chequer for half-an-hour. After all, Queenie had her all week!

A whack on the backside was enough to convince Chequer I meant business and, grudging every step, she sidled down the drive.

We had a fight at the end of the drive and at the point where I turned her off into the woods. It was exhausting and not at all the effortlessly floating ride I had imagined. I turned back after giving Chequer a chance to drink at the stream. She fairly flew down the track, stopping in a skid at the gate

Chequer was convinced I meant business

and then dancing about like a maniac while I struggled to shut it.

When I first heard Queenie's thin squeal I didn't quite believe my ears. Surely, we were too far from home. Chequer's head went up and she let out an ear-splitting neigh. Seconds later, Queenie appeared round the corner with four skinny legs flying in all directions as she slithered on the tarmac.

Dear God! I shut my eyes tight. She was still there when I opened them and Chequer was bounding up and down like a champagne cork ready to pop. With luck, I managed to get Queenie onto the verge side of the road then put Chequer into a striding trot.

I turned the pair of them into the field as soon as I got back to let them run off their nerves. The front lawn was covered in pockmarks and pansies thrown up by Queenie's hoofs. I shut my eyes. Dad would be livid.

"Susan!" Dad's voice boomed. I put the saddle down by the step and went into the kitchen. Mum was sitting on a stool, her face white. In one hand she held a glass of something. It trembled as she lifted it to her lips.

"That horse has to go!" she croaked. Queenie's frightened face swam before my eyes. "But who let her out?" I demanded. "What did you say?" asked Dad, using his pompous voice.

"Who let her out?" I repeated. "That's what I said. If mother's upset she's only herself to blame for interfering. Queenie could have been killed out there!"

"My fault!" cried Mum, and her eyebrows shot up as she finished whatever was in the glass in one gulp. "My fault!" she continued. "I don't know how you have the cheek after what you did. Cruel it was, separating them like that. A mother and her baby. If you had heard that poor thing - nearly broke the door down she did. I only went in to give her a bit of company. Thumped me in the stomach and barged past, the little beast."

"Well, it's your own fault," I told her. "You shouldn't have been in there. I told you to leave her."

"That's enough, Susan," snapped Dad. "They should not be kept like this. Out of sight, out of mind, you said. There's one sure way to see that they are - sell one!"

"No!" I exploded as my spirits dropped to zero.

"Yes!" Dad insisted and he meant it. "You can't go on playing with lives like this, Susan. If you insist on keeping them both you'll have to pay livery for

Queenie to be sent away and weaned properly. It's only fair."

Hot tears filled my eyes. I fled from the kitchen, muttering beneath my breath. Dad knew I would never be able to afford it! When I reached the field I collapsed onto the ground, beating it with my fists before bursting into tears. Ten minutes later I looked up to find Queenie and Chequer staring down at me. Their beautiful dark eyes were so soft and gentle I thought my heart would break.

I could avoid the truth no longer. Dad was right about me. I had been so selfish in my wish to find a way of keeping Chequer that I hadn't given a thought to the problems. It would take five years to make the sort of horse I wanted of Queenie and I knew that I just hadn't got the kind of patience that allows you to wait that long. I needed my horse right now.

Wiping tears from my eyes with the back of my hand, I walked back to the house to draft an advertisement for the Gazette. It was more important that I got a buyer who would give them a good home - both of them - than I got too good a price. I owed them that much at least.

As I counted out the money to pay for the advertisement, it struck me that this had been an expensive mistake all round. I'd spent a fortune feeding Queenie and lost six months' riding I could have had with Chequer before I should have needed to sell her. And only to learn that I wasn't as clever as I

thought after all. In the end, Dad had been right about me – one horse at a time was as much as I could manage.

Now I was here, leaning against the fence, watching my darling ponies and trying to stamp them onto my mind so that I would never forget them. Chequer raised her head as a car crunched onto the gravel drive. Mr. Brett and his daughter Jacqueline had come for a second look. My tears blurred Queenie's curious expression as she trotted up the field. I knew Mr.

Brett would buy, for Jacqueline had fallen for Chequer at first sight.

Biting my lip to hold back the tears, I forced my lips into a smile of welcome and turned to greet them. It was hard to be pleasant to the people who I knew would take my ponies away from me. It was painful to my pride too, because I could see that Jacqueline would give them a really good home, far better than mine, because for one thing she had more horse sense!

Privileged

As usual, it was raining. Nicola hunched her parka higher on her shoulders and thrust her hands deeper into the pockets. "Clipper'll love this!" she complained. Her cousin Deborah tried to cheer her up. "Maybe it'll brighten up by the time you go," she said, but although the cloud looked lighter, the rain was still heavy.

Nicola shrugged and gave a quick smile, saying: "Just as well we've been drawn early, or I'd have had to fit him webbed feet!"

By now they had reached the top of the slope and joined the knot of riders inspecting the course. They were considering the drop jump, with it's low take-off rail and two big steps down to the wooded track below. "I've seen worse!" shrugged Nicola.

"Doesn't it scare you?" asked Deborah, not believing her cousin could take it so calmly.

"No point in being frightened or you'll never get round," exclaimed Nicola. "It's no more dangerous than going for a car ride. At worst all that happens is you fall off, and broken arms don't take long to mend."

"What about Clipper?" asked Deborah with concern for Nicola's mount.

"Mum'll look after him for me," Nicola said. "Anyway, you can't ride round as if you expect the worst. That's asking for trouble. But you know Clipper, he'll jump anything you point him at. Don't worry, it doesn't look so bad when you're actually going round."

"If you say so," sighed Deborah, finding her cousin's enthusiasm hard to match. Maybe that was to be expected. Aunt Sarah had ridden since childhood and brought Nicola up on Pony Club and winter meets. Deborah's own mother thought that horses were

only good for fertilising the roses. It had taken Deborah two years to persuade her parents to buy her a pony and the one they'd chosen was as sensible as you could get – if the jump looked at all risky, Jasper refused to go near it.

Much as she loved Jasper, Deborah envied Nicola's luck in having Clipper. Jasper was not the type to encourage bravery in the face of a challenge though Nicola did have a point as far as falling off was concerned – nerves always took longer to heal than bruises.

There were another ten jumps to see after the drop. They arrived back at the box with hair like rats' tails. Aunt Sarah had taken off Clipper's bandages, brushed him over and left him tied up until the rain stopped.

Following her example, the girls scrambled into the cab of the box and Nicola pulled out her camera. She explained to Deborah in great detail how to use the telephoto switch so that she could get a good shot of Clipper taking the drop fence.

By the time Deborah had grasped how to work the black box, the rain had stopped and a watery sun was beginning to send thin beams of light across the park. Nicola did a last

Nicola pulled out her camera

minute check of her tack then saddled Clipper and backed him out. Once his feet touched the grass he was hopeless, gnashing his teeth and jumping about so it was almost impossible to tighten the girth. "Mind he doesn't nip!" warned Nicola as Deborah took the reins to steady the gelding. "He's not used to competitions and gets a bit above himself."

Deborah watched the pair jog and sidle their way to the open ground where fellow competitor Pam Holliday was quietly schooling her Hanoverian, Warcry. The black horse looked alert but attentive and Deborah couldn't help thinking Clipper ought to look a bit more like him just twenty minutes before his round.

She stayed to watch Nicola take the practice jump twice, then wished her cousin good luck and headed off to the spot over the hill from which she was to take the photograph.

The drop jump was popular with the spectators, if not with the riders, and it took a while for Deborah to find a place where she had a clear enough view for a good shot.

A rumbling noise turned all heads in one direction in time to see Warcry appear on the skyline. He looked huge. Deborah's heart leapt into her mouth

as the black horse jumped down, took a short stride and cleared the second element perfectly. A ripple of admiration stirred the crowd. Deborah found herself smiling, her own heart racing as if she had just taken the jump. Now she understood what Nicola meant about the thrill of conquering a difficult course.

There were three more horses clear before Nicola came on the horizon with Clipper pulling like a train. Deborah lifted the camera, praying the shutter would be quick enough to make up for the shaking of her hands. "Bit green, those two!" said a woman in the crowd.

It was Clipper's sudden hesitation she'd noticed. Through the camera his eyes bulged in horror at the sight of the vanishing slope. Grimly determined, Nicola rallied him with her heels and a shout of encouragement. Clipper teetered on the edge and then launched himself as the shutter clicked.

Deborah bit her lip in anticipation as she watched his hindlegs rap the take-off rail. She saw how he twisted to regain his balance, but came down badly with his near forleg skewing under him on the wet ground. Nicola catapulted over Clipper's head. The gelding rolled, somersaulting over the second jump as the crowd held its breath. Clipper landed with a nasty thudding sound.

For a moment there was a great stillness. Then Deborah slithered down the hill to Nicola's side. "She's my cousin!" she shouted to the steward who moved to stop her. Another official was there first to help Nicola to her feet. Her right arm was awkwardly twisted at the wrist.

With a heart-breaking whinny, Clipper struggled to his feet and stood

with one leg trailing miserably. The young steward caught Deborah's eye. His face was sad.

"The vet's on his way," he said quietly. "He'll do his best for him."

Silently Deborah helped her cousin up the hill into the arms of the St. John's Ambulance people. Then she fell back against one of the trees, fighting the urge to be sick. Sweat broke onto her brow and her legs were trembling as she let them give way and sat down heavily on the wet grass. Poor Nicola, she'd had such high hopes. But she had her confidence to help her through. Before long she'd forget and next year she'd be back to try again. Deborah could only hope the same would be true also of poor, brave Clipper.

That's What Friends are For

"Go on, Tina, come with us!" Lucy implored. She was kneeling with her arms wrapped around the seat headrest to steady herself as the bus swayed.

"It'll be great fun," Janet agreed, eyes bright with anticipation.

I looked at Tina. She was about to give in.

"Topper isn't clipped," I suggested, reminding Tina of the difference between her lovable, hairy thirteen hand pony and Lucy and Janet

111

Ridley's high-bred horses.

Tina sighed. "I'd love to Lucy but, well, Pat's right. Topper will get hot and he is on the small side."

"He can carry you easily," Lucy continued, not to be done out of her fun. "Lord Kendale will be there," Janet put in, "and young Michael." Tina went red and Lucy, herself going rather pink, began to giggle.

"I won't be out of place ...?" Tina began. "Of course not," laughed Lucy. "Don't let Patricia (*that's me, by the way*) put you off just because *her* pony's no good."

"Bobby's got more sense in his left ear than in your two ponies put together," I retorted hotly. "He does an important job. Yours are nothing more than fancy toys!"

Lucy exchanged a look with her sister. "Walking around the moor all day hardly calls for much skill," she remarked acidly, then disappeared behind her seat.

Tina turned away to stare out of the

window. I knew she had wanted to be friends with Lucy and Janet for ages. Their Anglo-Arabs, Sirocco and Callen, impressed her more than my Bobby, a five-year-old Dales gelding, ever could.

Now, I had spoiled her chances with them. More fool her, I thought angrily. Tina was stupid not to realise Janet and Lucy Ridley were only interested in her as a joke. She was no more up to appearing with the Kendale hounds than she was to run in the National.

Bobby was waiting for me at the

corner of his field and whickered in greeting. "Don't worry, Bob," I reassured him. "You don't need rosettes to prove your worth to me." He cocked an ear in response to my voice and pranced along the side of the hedge, kicking his heels high until he knew he'd made me laugh.

I'd had Bobby since the day he was born and we were very close. He always knew how to make me laugh, whether by giving me a playful buck, a mock chase with teeth bared, or sneakily pulling my shirt out of my trousers.

Bobby worked on the farm alongside his dam, Jeannie. They carried hay up to the intakes and took my father across the boggy moorland to check over his sheep. Both ponies had developed a canny knack of knowing exactly where the flock were to be found.

The snow started during the night and by next morning a thick carpet lay over the yard and drifted high against

That's What Friends are For

The two stout ponies were invaluable

the buildings. Riding up to the top fields with hay for the sheep was an unpleasant task. As the wind whipped my cheeks, I had one amusing thought to warm me. Lucy and Janet's ponies had been oated up for a day's hunting. I'd have given anything to see them mount up for exercise on Sunday morning. Callen was explosive at the best of times.

By the following morning, the snow had stopped but the wind was just as strong. It howled round the house and rattled the doors and windows. Dad was thinking about bringing the sheep closer to the house. Mum was getting out candles in case a power-line came down. For once, I was lingering over my homework, glad for an excuse not to go outside.

The phone rang. I answered it in my best voice, expecting to hear Aunt Grace at the other end asking if we were coming down to tea. She never seemed to realise the difference it made to our weather, being twenty miles out of town and stuck on the moorside.But it was Tina who spoke.

Her voice was shrill and barely recognizable. "Oh, Pat, Topper's got out!" she sobbed and I could hear her

gulping down her tears.

"What's happened?" I asked.

There was a sniff as Tina struggled to control herself. "The storm last night ... blew part of the fence down ... the roof was ripped off the shelter ... Topper bolted and he's out on the moor."

Visions of little Topper in a snow-drift sprang to my mind as quickly as they had to my friend.

"Do you know which way he went?" I asked.

"Out by Howlbeck," said Tina. "I tried to trace him . . . but the drifts . . . I lost track."

"Bobby will find him," I assured her. "You set out from Whinney Banks and I'll come over from this side. You know Bob, he's got a nose like a bloodhound!" Tina sounded comforted by this. She thanked me and put the telephone down.

I wish I could have felt as certain. Bobby knew the habits of our sheep, but that was not the same as finding one bedraggled pony on a thousand acres of open moorland.

After two miles of steady plodding through snow that sometimes could be six inches or three feet deep, my toes were numb. I folded my arms to keep my fingers warm and gave Bobby a free rein to pick his way. Thank goodness Topper had not been clipped

or in this weather he wouldn't have stood a chance.

The white landscape seemed to go on for ever. If we didn't find Topper soon, I knew we would have to turn back. It could turn stormy quickly if the wind got up again and it was a long ride back home.

Suddenly, Bobby stopped, his head high and ears pricked. He let out a loud whinny. We both strained to hear an answer. The response was feeble, but it was there.

119

Bobby ploughed on quickly now, driving a wide track behind him. As we dropped into the gulley Topper appeared – cold, wet and shivering. I jumped down, haltered his ice-spiked face and covered him with the blanket from beneath Bobby's saddle.

Tina met us a mile down the moor. She ran forward, floundering through the snow and with tears streaming down her pale cheeks. Assured of her pony's safety Tina turned her attention to Bobby and produced two delicious but rather squashed mince pies.

"You're right, Patricia," she said, as she affectionately stroked Bobby's nose. "Bob may not be in the ribbons but he's the cleverest, bravest horse in the world." I grinned, slapping my pony's neck. Bobby merely nudged Tina's pocket for another mince pie.

The Expert

"For goodness sake, Sara, get your hands up and stop sawing at him!" Grimly, Sara Freeman picked her hands off the grey gelding's withers. Her mouth was pressed tight and her cheeks flushed with anger. Did her mother have to tell the whole showground whenever she saw something to criticise? Mrs. Freeman stood at the collecting ring rail. Booted feet apart, gloved hands sunk deep inside the pockets of her waxed jacket, she looked every bit the trainer.

After all, it wasn't as if Sara was some numbskull beginner. She had been riding for six years now and won fifty rosettes with Basil – at least she would have done by the end of today. Assuming the begging dog pose, so beloved by the modern teacher, Sara put Basil at the practice jump. He sailed over, but then it wasn't surprising with the jump at only three foot three.

The loudspeaker called for the first competitor in the under fourteen-two jumping and Mrs. Freeman hurried away. She would return in ten minutes to inform her daughter how to ride the course. Sara pulled a face – it never occurred to mother that she might be able to work it out herself.

Caroline Bates rode over as Sara walked her pony down the row of parked boxes. As usual, her palomino Floss was above himself. He was sweating like a Derby winner and kept snatching his bit in an irritating fashion. "He's getting worse, not

better," said Caroline. "Do you think your mother might have some ideas about what to do?"

"I'm sure she will, but I can't guarantee they'll be of any use," grunted Sara.

"She was right last time," said Caroline dutifully, "about the bit being too low and banging his teeth." Sara fumed and said: "You don't have to live with her criticising all the time!"

"She's only trying to help," smiled

Caroline. "Show off you mean,"
snapped Sara, "and make me look
stupid." Caroline pulled Floss to a
fidgety halt. "At least she takes an
interest," she insisted. "You ought to
think yourself lucky."

Interested, yes, she was certainly
that thought Sara. Ever since they
swopped Gemini for Basil, a bigger
pony with a jumping record, mother
had *really* taken an interest. She'd
ridden Basil so much that he was
beginning to think he was *her* pony. It
was time to go back to the collecting
ring. Seeing Caroline at the rail with
her mother, Sara hung back until it
was her turn to ride and then trotted
straight into the main ring.

The course was well within their
capabilities. Basil took the jumps
steadily and easily as if he wanted to
show the other ponies how it ought to
be done. They came out without
needing a word of advice from mother
and Sara couldn't stop grinning.
However, Mrs. Freeman met her in the

collecting ring and launched straight in with directions for the jump off.

"Steven Warren's clear, the rest are on four and eight faults," she explained. "You'll need to go pretty fast to beat him, Sara, but don't cut the corner into the wall. It's at a funny angle and

needs a straight approach." Sara nodded, though she disagreed. A novice might need the extra stride, but she and Basil could manage without it. A moment later they were going over the practice jump and turning to the ring. Then, she forgot everything but the desire to win.

The starting markers were to the right. Sara put Basil into a steady canter, lined up the first jump then pushed him on. They flew over the rustic poles, landing on the turn to take the broad oxer at speed. As she came down, Basil stretched out and stood back to take the bright yellow planks in style. They skimmed the corner and raced over the double. Then there was a long stretch to the wall. Sara pushed Basil faster and turned him sharply into it.

She was too close – she knew it even as she shot over the pony's head. An excited "Ooh!" went up from the crowd as Sara smashed through the red wall.

Pain in the chest doubled her over. Basil, she saw through misty eyes, had been returned. Sara forced herself upright, took a deep breath and swallowed hard against the dizziness that swept over her. Then she was being boosted into the saddle and

She knew she was too close!

facing the wall for a second time.
Going straight with plenty of space
they cleared it easily. As he landed,
Basil pulled for the treble and a sharp
pain shot up Sara's arm. The reins
slipped and the pony took off, hurdling
the first parts and cat-jumping the last.
He only stopped when they almost ran
into another horse in the collecting
ring.

"Sara, are you all right?" called
Mother. "You look ghastly!" added
Caroline with some concern. "Get
down and go over to the first-aid
people," ordered Mrs. Freeman "I'll see
to Basil."

"No, I'm fine," claimed Sara, who
just could not bear to see her mother on
Basil. "You don't look it," wailed
Caroline. "Well I am," snapped Sara
and turned Basil away, forcing her
right hand to take hold of the rein.

Sara might have been able to avoid
the show ring ambulance, but she
could not escape her sprained wrist. By
evening it had swelled alarmingly,

making a tennis-ball lump on the back of her hand. "Do you think it's broken?" she asked.

Mrs. Freeman prodded the swelling tentatively with one finger and consulted the anatomy book on her lap. "I don't think it can be," she said. "You rode all right afterwards. You could move everything couldn't you?" "For a few minutes," Sara replied, wiggling her fingers experimentally. They all worked, but not much. "How long will it be like this?" Mrs. Freeman thought a week, maybe ten days, but warned she might have to rest it or it could take months to recover properly.

"But it's Skelby Show on Saturday," moaned Sara. "I can't just leave Basil until then." Her mother's words of comfort were not the ones Sara wished to hear. "I'll keep Basil going for you, you've no need to worry over that," was her mother's promise.

But Sara did worry. Even though she couldn't ride herself, she did not like to see her mother riding Basil. It might have been easier if mother had been a rotten rider, thought Sara, but to see them cantering immaculate figure eights forced her to admit that her mother was good, very good. Her seat was steadier than Sara's, her hands lighter. Basil didn't lean on her or drag the reins.

That week her mother looked different, younger somehow, and she was obviously enjoying the riding. She talked to the pony as she dismounted now to put up trotting poles. Yet she had never bought a horse of her own ... Sara's brow puckered as she watched her mother ride Basil over the poles and clear the wide triple bar she had set up. She saw the quality in his stride and suddenly understood. Her mother had put all her money into

buying Sara a good pony and had probably hoped she herself would be given a chance to exercise it, longed for it even.

Sara bit her lip. She'd begrudged her mother every minute spent with the horse. Tears filled her eyes as she remembered how glad she had been of her mother's help with the first ponies.

Yet Basil... he had made mother a rival in her eyes. She had been jealous because Basil showed her how good her mother really was and she did not like to feel inferior. Caroline had been right, she did undervalue her mother. Where would she be with a stay-at-home mother like Mrs. Bates? Throwing a cardigan around her shoulders, Sara pulled on her boots and ran out as her mother was about to set up a new jump.

"I'll change them," Sara called. "Save you getting off." Mrs. Freeman swung from the saddle anyway. "It's easier if we do things together, " she laughed out loud. Sara caught her eye and smiled. "Yes," she replied. "Yes, it is."

Cloudburst

"**C**ome on, Pepper! Let's get moving!" cried Samantha. The cloud burst she had hoped to avoid made fat splashmarks on Samantha's anorak as she pushed her pony into canter. Beneath Pepper's hoofs, the verge squelched and he began to slither as the road dipped to take them down from the moor.

"Steady on!" Samantha called, pulling back on reins that were slipping through her fingers. 'The rate you're going we'll end up flat on our backs!" The pony broke stride and trotted, bouncing and slipping, eager to get back to the warmth of his stable. Dark shapes came out of the mist as a group of hill ponies cut across their track to make for the high ground and the shelter of Ikleigh Tor rocks. Samantha patted Pepper's neck. "Glad you're not with them any more," she told him. "Bet you wouldn't like to be left out here in this weather."

Pepper saw the gate that would take them off the moor and stretched his neck before coming to a bone-jolting halt. The catch was stiff so Samantha jumped off and led Pepper through. He jibbed and kept swinging into her as she fumbled for the loop, her fingers stiffening in the cold wet of the rain. By the time she remounted, the saddle was running with water and the downpour had lost its excitement. The chill seeped under her collar and through jodhpurs that stuck to the saddle every time she sat down.

Pepper raced down the High Street,

Dark shapes came out of the mist

his head bent low against the rain, knowing exactly when to turn to Ellots Farm. Soon they were striding down the steep, rutted track and the rain didn't seem quite so bad because they were almost home. Samantha opened the gate from the saddle and swung Pepper in. He fidgeted and spun away, sliding through the mud in his hurry to reach shelter.

The little barn was like a world apart. Samantha patted Pepper's neck as she tied him in his stall. She always thought it a shame that he could not have the whole of the ground floor to wander in now that the sheep were out, but there was no telling when Mr. Chard was going to bring feed and hay down to store. So, she continued to put Pepper in his own stall with the tack next to it, beneath a couple of sacks.

"Never mind, eh, Pepper?" Samantha said, as she rubbed him down with a handful of straw. "At least you are out of the rain now."

She pulled an extra wad from the

bale to make him a good warm bed and filled a generous haynet. Before she opened the door to the wind, Samantha glanced back at her pony one more time. The sight of Pepper on his deep bed, chewing contentedly, made her feel all warm inside. He was so much better off than those poor things they had seen on the moor without even a feed to look forward to. Samantha shut the door and hunched her shoulders as she climbed the wet slope to the gate.

"For heaven's sake, Samantha,"

cried her mother. "Look at the state you're in! You're wet through! Get those clothes stripped off and yourself into a bath before you catch your death!"

Samantha smiled as she heaved off her riding boots. Normally, her mother would have crowned her for coming in so filthy but today, with the dirty clothes wet, her maternal instinct got the better of her. She even took Samantha a mug of hot chocolate to sip in the bathroom.

The rain was still hard at it when the family sat down to tea two hours later. The television news droned on from the corner about inches of rainfall, over awful films of water swirling into people's front rooms and caravans floating down rivers.

"I'm glad we're not down in the valley," Samantha's mother commented as she watched a family from Cornwall climbing into a boat moored in their front garden. "Knew what they were doing when they built Ikleigh on a ridge, they did." She glanced at the window. "The bulbs will be swept out to sea at the rate it's coming down - won't be many daffies poking their heads up in the spring."

Samantha smiled to herself. Her mother was so daft about daffodils that she'd fill the garden with them given a chance. Spring was the only time she ever took an interest in Pepper. She would walk down through his field to reach the daffodil banks along the side of the river. Samantha's smile vanished, the paste sandwich halfway to her mouth. Walking down the field to the river ... the river that bordered Pepper's field!

Samantha leapt from the table. "Just where do you think you're off to?" her mother asked sharply. "I've got to check Pepper is all right," exclaimed Samantha.

"Samantha, you'll get soaked!" called her mother, but Samantha was already out of sight as she cried out: "I have to go! What if the river bursts its banks?"

What if it already had, Samantha thought to herself as she wrestled her way into wellingtons and a soggy anorak. Seconds later she had dragged her bicycle out of the shed and was tearing down the High Street. On the track to Ellots Farm she stood on the pedals, bumping and bouncing over ruts and stones. Swerving round the high hedge to the field gate Samantha stopped suddenly, her mouth falling open in amazement.

*Sometimes she stood on the pedals, bumping
and bouncing*

The river had come up way beyond its bank. It swirled against the alder trees and sucked at the stone walls of the barn. Heart pounding, Samantha dropped the bicycle and raced down the slope. She slithered and slid out of control but with only one thought in her mind – to get Pepper out!

Tears mingled with the rain on her face. How could she have been so stupid not to think of the river! With all the rain, she should have guessed there would be floods.

The bottom of the field was already a foot deep and the water slowed her progress. It swept round her legs and up over the tops of her boots, making them heavy and difficult to move. As she waded further in, the undertow began to pull, dragging at her feet as soon as they left the slippery mud. Three steps, two, one step more ... Samantha's fingers closed thankfully over the cold iron bolts and pulled them back. Pepper gave a frightened neigh. "It's all right, Pep," she called to him.

Samantha ploughed on as straw and bits of wood swirled up into the water and out of the door. Her feet slipped as she reached for the stalls and for one horrible moment she was under water. Pepper began to thrash about in panic. Coughing and spluttering, Samantha groped into the dim barn, talking all the time. Pepper hardly seemed to recognize her, he was panicking so much and tugging madly at the halter rope.

The first chance she got, Samantha slid past him and unclipped the rope. Pepper sprang back suddenly, his hindlegs slipping beneath him, water flying in all directions. Then, he fled out of the door with ears laid flat against his head.

Weary and suddenly feeling very cold, Samantha sloshed out after him. He had gone straight for the gate, where the hedge was thickest. His head was up and he kept skittering around, not yet trusting her. His tail hung in a fat, wet strand between his legs and his coat was plastered flat.

"Poor Pepper!" she almost sobbed. Samantha reached into her pocket and found a packet of mints amongst the mush of pony nuts. This reassured Pepper and the shaking of panic became a shivering of cold. "You would have been better on the moor after all, wouldn't you?" Samantha said. She stroked his neck and wondered if her parents would let her put the pony in the garage to dry off. Tears pushed out from beneath her lids. Away from the herd, tied up in a barn, Pepper had been trapped and couldn't be expected to fend for himself.

It had been a nasty shock to remind her just how big a responsibility owning a pony could be – and how her forgetfulness had very nearly cost Pepper his life.

Not a Novice Ride

Parkview Popinjay was a truly beautiful animal. Her clean limbs tapered to small dark feet. She stood absolutely square, raising her tail and putting an arch in her neck. On all her copper coat there was not a single white hair. "Do you like her, Vanessa?" my father asked. "She's lovely," I told him delightedly.

"Three-quarter Thoroughbred, quarter Welsh. Your first taste of a blood horse. Done very well in hand, and Mrs. Gordon broke her herself," explained my father, adding: "She's five in July!"

Thank goodness! At least she would be able to jump this season. What did I want with a green horse that was too immature to win anything? At times like this I wished my old pony, Kingpin, could have grown with me. Kingpin was fourteen when I got him, old by most people's standards, but he was fast and he knew the game. We collected ninety rosettes and three cups in our first show season. Now I was fifteen, and Kingpin had been sold. Parkview Popinjay was Kingpin's replacement. But would she be good enough?

"Aren't you going to try her out, Vanessa?" Daddy sounded anxious. "Mrs. Gordon assured me she's a lovely ride. Keep a good hold on her though. She's only been hacked six months." He smiled, saying: "Not a novice ride, but I'm sure you'll master her."

By the time I had changed into jodhpurs and boots, Daddy had saddled Popinjay and she stood lipping his pockets for titbits. I didn't like the sign. I wanted a pony like King, full of spirit, impressive to ride - and to watch. Nevertheless, I waved and smiled to Daddy as I turned down the field. There might be a bit of spirit in her somewhere, and if I found it, I knew I could get her going.

I urged Popinjay into a trot as we turned down the long side of the field. The slope unbalanced her. She began to run. Speed bred speed. With growing excitement, I felt her snatch at the bit. She skidded round the bottom corner, sprang into canter, and flew up the field.

My father waved, pointing to the jump he had set up for me. Dragging down on one rein, I turned her into the flight of rustics. She ran at them, then baulked and tried to stop. I dug in my heels and she cleared the fence with room to spare. A tight turn brought her snorting and prancing to my father's side.

"How do you like her?" Daddy asked

I dug in my heels and she cleared the fence

as we turned the mare out.

"She's got spirit," I agreed, "but her tack needs changing. All this head tossing – she wants a martingale and a kimblewick would help. I can hold her in a snaffle at the moment but once she gets some feed inside her ..."

"That's our Vanessa!" Daddy chuckled. "I'm glad to see you aren't afraid of a horse with a bit of spirit."

I rode Popinjay out most nights after school, concentrating on her jumping or gymkhana games. She was fast, but not sure like Kingpin. She got carried away with herself and refused to turn or go near the flags I had made.

Still, she was improving and when I increased her concentrates she was soon brimming with energy. People stood to one side when we trotted down the street. Popinjay certainly got herself noticed.

If I'd had the sense to admit it, I would have known something was wrong. Even with the martingale and new bit, Popinjay was a handful. She pulled like a train. She was anxious to please. She couldn't get round the jumps fast enough, but I wouldn't face up to the fact that she needed more quiet schooling than Kingpin. More than once she took off with me and I only just managed to stop before we reached the main road. The truth was, I could barely control her.

Lingby Show was to be Popinjay's debut. I'd never bothered with it before, but it would be an excellent place to try her out. We were all right until we got within sight of the show field. Then, Popinjay went berserk. She sidled and bucked, spooked at cars and buckets, and tried to run off with every horse that passed her.

Julia, my friend from riding school days, was there on her stolid dun pony, Chester. She saw me and waved. One thing in Popinjay's favour, I thought as I watched Chester approach, was that she did prove my skill as a rider. Chester looked as though any beginner could handle him.

"Is this your new pony?" asked Julia admiringly. "She's lovely!"

I nodded, too occupied in holding Popinjay to risk conversation.

"Don't you get tired of her carrying on like that?" asked Julia.

"No," I lied. "I like a pony with spirit. She's a great ride."

My cheeks blushed as I saw the disbelief in Julia's face. I had to prove I could handle Popinjay in spite of her disobedience, or Julia would tell everyone my pony was too much for me. "I was just going to try the Clear Round jumping," I went on, turning to Julia. "Do you want to watch?"

"If you like," shrugged Julia. I didn't like it at all but I was determined to prove Julia wrong.

Popinjay saw the coloured poles and threw up her head. She danced on the spot, dragging at the reins. Then she was away, running madly at the first jump, taking off miles in advance and sending the top pole flying. The ring was very small and Popinjay was going very fast. I hauled her round to face the second obstacle. She slithered. She stopped. The red and white poles were suddenly very close and then I was crashing through them. The ground hit me hard.

My parents were waiting at the entrance. Mummy's face was pale with fright, but my father's cheeks burned in anger. "Damned pony!" he fumed. "Could've killed you!"

"Where is she?" I stammered, scanning the field for my copper-coloured horse, suddenly afraid for her. "Julia has caught her," Mummy reassured.

And so she had. Popinjay shivered and steamed, hugging Chester's side for comfort. I knew when I saw her that it had all been my fault. I had wanted too much and I wasn't prepared to work for it. I was too vain to ride a pony like Chester, but I wasn't good enough for Popinjay.

My father patted my shoulder. "We'll get rid of her. You deserve something better Vanessa," he said.

"No!" I replied. "Let's give her another chance." Or rather, I thought, let's hope she is forgiving enough to grant *me* another chance.

He Just lay Shuddering

Twenty metre circle at working trot, rising, transition to walk at the red marker - well, rusty red can - then down the centre at the midpoint of the short side and perform a square halt beside the clump of thistles. As I closed my legs to Tarquin's sides and felt on the reins, my bay pony came to a standstill. I sat a moment reaching into the saddle, concentrating on the feel of his back, searching for the kink of a ragged hindleg.

"You are supposed to bow," Donna

called from the fence. "The judges won't like it if you just sit there like a stuffed duck."

I nodded smartly and let Tarquin walk out on a loose rein. Donna only had time to make jokes when everything was going well, so Tarquin's performance must have been as good as it felt. "He went better this time, didn't he?" I ventured with a grin.

Tarquin's preparation for the dressage test had been so thorough he should have been able to do it on his own by now. If he behaved as well as this tomorrow, I would have no complaints.

Deborah had agreed to pick me up on Sunday morning. Tarquin would be boxed alongside Donna's own Pippa, a solid Dales mare, and her sister Sheena's eleven-two pony, Dainty. Her father's old cattle transporter had been converted for the occasion with wooden partitions, roll-topped with coconut matting.

I stabled Tarquin early on Saturday

evening, brushing him until his bay coat shone like silk. His white socks were shampooed and dried and I laid him a thick bed for the night to help keep him clean. His night rug would keep off most of the dirt, so with luck I would have little to do in the morning. I hurried to change and wash my hair ready for the Youth Club Disco.

My mother wasn't very keen on me going out, but as it was a Valentine dance and also I had got everything ready for the morning, she didn't feel able to stop me. Dad drove me over to the Disco but happily gave up his duty of providing a lift home when I was promised a ride back with Zöe and Karen. All the better for me, since they weren't leaving until midnight.

Sunday morning! Mum woke me up at eight with a cup of hot tea. As my brain was two hours out after the late night, I suppose it wasn't surprising that I fell asleep the moment she shut the door. The next time I opened my eyes a skin had formed on the tea and the clock insisted it was five-to-nine.

I sneaked out of the front door so Mum wouldn't see me and rushed over to the stable. Tarquin got a quick brush over. I measured out his breakfast and dashed back to the house with no-one the wiser.

But time moves in fits and starts when you are in a hurry and the ten minutes I saved in the stables soon vanished. Suddenly it was twenty-past-nine and I was still in my stable clothes with hair unbrushed. To top it

I had slept far too long!

all, Donna arrived five minutes early and I had to fetch Tarquin while still pulling on my sweater and trying to cram my tie into a jodhpur pocket.

Donna and her father lowered the wide ramp while I ran for Tarquin's saddle and bridle. Thankfully he had always been an easy pony to box. I led him in with his night rug on, tossed a bag of grooming kit in with the rest and secured his halter on a long rope.

"Don't you want to bandage him!" asked Donna with some surprise. "We can wait – it won't take five minutes."

Mr. Evans looked fretfully at his watch, his glance warning me that we were already behind time. Tarquin stood square in his stall, looking content. It was only ten minutes' drive to Otherby Farm. "He'll be all right," I called back to Donna. "It's not far."

When we arrived I ran down to the Secretary's tent to pick up our numbers while Mr. Evans and Donna unboxed the ponies. Mr. Evans was in a hurry as he had some beef cattle to pick up at ten o'clock that morning.

The moment I turned back up the hill and saw Sheena running towards me I knew something was wrong. Her little face was chalk white. She was only trying to spare me, I suppose, when she insisted I stayed away but I was

already sprinting for the box. I saw Donna lead Dainty down the ramp. The little mare's coat was dark and wet, her eyes white-rimmed. Deborah wouldn't look at me and I knew why when I reached the box.

Pippa's head was in the air. Her

nostrils flared, red-centred. Weak-kneed, I mounted the ramp.

Tarquin's hindfeet were dripping blood. They stuck awkwardly through the rough partition, suspended on the splintered wood. Mr. Evans was slicing at the halter rope with a thick penknife. "Lucky you racked him loose," he said, "or else he'd have broken his neck."

Tears choked me. Tarquin lay wide eyed, shivering. His body was twisted, with hindfeet through the shattered partition and his knees twisted under him. His shoulders were wedged against Pippa's buckled stall. "Must have slipped at a corner," explained Mr.Evans. "Hindfeet shot through the wood. Wouldn't have been able to get up again. Lucky he didn't panic."

Mr. Evans pulled the partition away while I held Tarquin's legs. He did not struggle, but just lay shuddering with sweat sliding from his coat. "We had better see if he can stand," said Mr. Evans and, from his tone, I knew he thought the worst. But Tarquin struggled bravely to his feet. Rocking a little, he stood square, burying his head in my shoulder.

Donna led a shaken but unhurt Pippa down the ramp and Tarquin followed gingerly, sticking close to my side. Sheena was sent to fetch the Club vet and Tarquin was give the official okay. The cuts looked worse than they were and his rug had saved his body from more than a few bruises.

I did not get off so lightly. The other Riding Club members refused to speak to me when they heard about what had happened. And one thing is for sure – no matter how short the journey I will always put on the bandages!

Saturday Afternoons

"**D**o hurry up, Beth, or the meter will be into the red!" called Mrs. Wallace. "Coming!" her daughter Bethanie replied, glaring at her mother's back as she humped the heavy box of groceries higher against her chest. Mrs. Wallace strode away, her high-heeled Spanish boots clicking a regular tattoo upon the pavement. Her tailored coat billowed behind her as Bethanie was falling further behind.

A turning car forced Mrs. Wallace to break stride. Bethanie put her chin down and forged ahead. She imagined herself a plough horse turning for home but, before she had made more than a few yards up, her mother was off again. Mrs. Wallace's head was high, chestnut hair streaming across her shoulders beneath a wide-brimmed hat that could only have stayed secure through the miracle of her amazing will power.

Mrs. Wallace stopped to load the car and then skillfully navigated their way into Knightsbridge. A few minutes later they were crossing Hyde Park. Beth squinted through the trees. At first she could see only cyclists and joggers. Then came a different movement, the unmistakable rhythm of a steady trot as a massive bay ridden by a uniformed soldier came into view. Further on, they passed two grey ponies with fine heads and incredibly thin legs. Each was backed by a smartly turned out child. Their teacher rode between them on a long-backed roan mare. Marble Arch passed by and the whole wonderful scene was over until the following Saturday afternoon.

When they got back home, Bethanie went upstairs to curl up on her bed with a horsy magazine, but even that did not cheer her today. It was nice to learn about ponies but saddening to think that she'd never be able to put the knowledge to any use. When the hall clock chimed a noisy half-past-five, Bethanie went downstairs to make some tea – always a good ploy when she wanted to sweeten her mother's mood.

"Bethie! You are a dear!" Mrs. Wallace enthused when her daughter appeared with the tea tray. She was sitting at the far end of the lounge, sorting through a pile of bills. Bethanie ought to have recognised this as a sign not to proceed, but she was too desperate to stop.

"Have you thought about it yet?" Bethanie asked at last. "About what, dear?" asked her mother. "Riding lessons," urged Beth. "You remember, I

was telling you how Hannah goes to Epping Forest every Saturday."

"And I told you that it was fifteen miles away." Rowena Wallace put down her cup and looked at her daughter squarely in the face. "Let's not have a scene over this, Bethie. I've told you before the answer is 'no'. Lessons are expensive and a waste of money. After all, we could never have a pony."

"But if we moved ..." spluttered Beth.

"Darling!" exclaimed Mrs. Wallace "Your Daddy works in London. This is our home." She raised a smile. "When I was your age I wanted to give up ballet lessons and become a canoeist. Your Grandma wouldn't let me and I've been thankful to her ever since – my skin would have been ruined! You'll be glad too when you are older. London is a great place to be."

Except when you want to ride, Bethanie thought. She took her tea into the next room and switched on the television. There was no point arguing with her mother. You might as well ask a zebra to change its stripes. She didn't understand that it wasn't a fad. In that way they were alike. Bethanie was as determined to ride as her mother had been to do her own thing.

"Fancy a working trip to Windsor on Saturday?" Mr. Wallace asked his wife when he came in from the studio later that week. "Super, darling!" Mrs. Wallace stood on tiptoe to kiss her husband's cheek before dashing to the kitchen to rescue the trout. "All day?" she asked over her shoulder. "These photo sessions usually are," he told her. "Of course, it is an early start. Eight o'clock away as we need the right light on the park for the photographs."

"Oh, well," sighed Mrs. Wallace, "Bethie and I will spend the day with Geraldine."

Beth heard and her heart dropped like a stone. Not only would she miss her one chance of seeing the horses in the park as usual, but she would have to sit in Geraldine's chic boutique listening to the two women discuss Paris fashion and Italian opera.

"Couldn't I stay behind?" Beth asked, wondering if she could fix up to spend the day with Hannah and go with her to Epping Stables. "But, darling," exclaimed her mother, "Geraldine will be so looking forward to seeing you. No, you come along with us."

"Are you ready?" Beth's mother appeared at the bedroom door wearing fancy knit leg-warmers over black-ribbed tights, a long sweater and genuine Balmoral boots. She gave a sigh of resignation at the sight of Bethanie's sweat-shirt and blue jeans, then tottered downstairs adding that she should hurry up!

Just as they were about to leave, the telephone rang. Mr. Wallace dashed back inside. A few moments later he appeared at the door, waving his wife back to the house. Bethanie watched her mother's face show surprise, shock

and disapproval but eventually some sort of agreement. Beth's father gave her a smile as they got back into the car. "Terry's model's got chicken pox," he explained. "We've got to call at Bayton Park first."

Once they were out of town, Bethanie pulled herself closer to the window and began looking out for horses. She could get that much at least out of the day. Along the Windsor road she spied three mares. Their wobbly-legged foals were busy chasing each other round their field. Beth became so engrossed in their antics she did not notice the car slow and turn off the main road, until a tall brick wall cut the foals from view.

They stopped in an old stableyard. Beth's eyes grew wider and wider. Aristocratic heads poked over every door. Here was a black thoroughbred, there a delicate dappled show pony. Terry Shaw, the photographer, then appeared from what Bethanie took to be a tack room. The make-up girl Liz followed, carrying a pair of cream jodhpurs over one arm. A short exchange took place between Terry, Beth's father and a dragon of a woman whose frown was deep enough to make her look most forbidding.

Mr. Wallace came back to the car and slid his seat forward. "Come out a minute, Bethie," he said. "I'm still not sure about this, John," Bethie's mother put in. Bethanie scrambled out, running her tongue over dry lips. She was going to be allowed to see the horses, maybe touch them.

"Are you sure the girl's going to be up to this?" asked the dragon-woman, who was introduced to Bethanie as Mrs. Drew, of Ridgeway Riding Clothes. "Absolutely!" Beth's father told her with enthusiasm. "Bethanie loves horses." "Right, let's get started," said Terry, rubbing his hands together.

"Just a moment!" The drama-trained voice of Beth's mother stopped everyone, including the thoroughbred who was trying to reach Terry's camera strap. "No one has asked Bethanie if she wants to do it." Mrs. Wallace crouched beside her daughter and explained: "They want you to stand in for the model, darling. If you don't want to do it, say so!"

Bethanie looked at the dapple-grey. Ponies were bigger in real life and she couldn't help feeling just a bit frightened. "It's just sitting, isn't it?" she whispered.

Her mother's eyes softened. "Yes, darling, just sitting and smiling for hours and hours. You'll get bored, but you'll look super and if you enjoy it I suppose we could consider getting you some training for some action shots next year."

So it had turned out a super Saturday for Beth after all.

174

For Want of a Saddle

"**C**laire! Answer the door will you? I'm up to my elbows in flour." In response to her mother's call, Claire Sterston put the box of decorations down, took her stick from the back of the chair and made her way into the hallway. Her legs were stiff this afternoon, especially the right one. In six months since her riding accident she had almost forgotten what it was like to walk normally.

Lisa Ryan was on the step, her face hidden behind a red scarf and a woolly hat pulled down over her brows. "Cold isn't it!" Lisa exclaimed, stripping off two pairs of gloves. "We'll have snow for Christmas." Lisa followed her friend into the hall. "Your leg still bad?" she asked as they reached the sitting room.

Claire nodded. "Mum says I've been overdoing things."

"You know, I've always like Red Hall," said Lisa as she sat down in front of the roaring log fire. "It's so homely, you'd never think it was haunted."

"What!" Claire's eyes opened wide.

Lisa grinned mischievously. "You mean you haven't heard? Well, it is only a rumour. I've never seen anything. Don't take it seriously, Claire. What I really came round for was to ask a favour, not scare you. Mum's got it into her head for us to spend Christmas with Gran, in Nottingham and everyone's got to go – no arguments."

"What about Topper?" asked Claire.

For the Want of a Saddle

Lisa settled down in front of the log fire

"I was coming to that," explained Lisa. "Would you keep an eye on her here? She wouldn't be any trouble – stays out most of the time. I'll make up a box for her, but there'll be no mucking out. I'd do all that when I got back."

Claire dropped onto a chair, wincing as she knocked her leg. A horse again at Red Hall! She had vowed there would never be another after Pearl, not after the accident. Lisa plucked anxiously at her woollen tights. "I wouldn't ask you normally, Claire. I know how you feel, but Topper's such a touchy old thing and you're the only one she trusts."

Claire chewed her lip. Topper was a sensitive mare. She would fret elsewhere. "Okay!" she finally blurted out. Life was much busier with Topper on the place. Morning and evening Claire tidied her bed and changed her water, then gave a small feed and some hay.

"Not finding that horse too much, are you?" Mr. Sterston asked one

evening when Claire nodded to sleep in front of the television. "It's just the excitement of Christmas," smiled Claire, knowing it was really the memories Topper's presence had awoken within her. She longed to ride again, but knew it would never happen. Claire was remembering how Doctor Blake used to come round to look at her leg. He would make her stretch and bend it, then check the colourful swellings around the knee. His fingers felt strange, as if she could only feel with half of the nerves and the middle of her leg was jelly.

"When will I be able to get up?" Claire had asked as the support bandages were replaced.

The doctor's mouth widened into a faint smile. "A couple of weeks yet!" he'd told her.

Always more time to wait. When she lay back and closed her eyes they thought she had gone to sleep. They left the door open and spoke louder than they might have done. "Don't put too much hope on it, Mrs. Sterston," Claire heard Doctor Blake say. " The way that joint has locked she'll be lucky to walk again, never mind ride."

Claire blinked and yawned. "I think I'll turn in," she said. Upstairs she soon fell into a deep yet troubled sleep of dreams . . .

Claire dreamed of a plastic sack flapping dully in the hedge. Pearl was all over the road. Beyond the blind corner a lorry rumbled. "Pearl!" Claire heaved on the reins . . . to her surprise she next saw not a grey neck, but smooth chestnut stretching in front of her. The road had vanished and they were galloping across country. Hoof-beats thundered around her. " Elizabeth, don't!" She turned in the saddle, not surprised for some reason that someone

called her by a strange name. A red-coated rider with a handlebar moustache was waving shouting: "It's too high, go to the right!" The chestnut mare pulled eagerly. She could clear the hedge with ease. As for cousin Gerald,

he was always treating her like bone-
china. Her hand slid forward, giving
the mare her head as they launched
themselves at the hedge. They hestitated
in mid-flight as the landing side
dropped sickeningly into blackness ...

Next, lorry brakes squealed. There
was a stench of burning rubber. Claire
felt Pearl's hindlegs slip and the
ground came up hard as they skewed
into a ditch ... the scene changed ...

Voices and faces swam through the
darkness of Claire's dream. "Oh
Elizabeth! You would never listen!" a
strange Mama lamented. Even the
warm glow of the oil lamp couldn't
mask the whiteness of her face. Her
fingers clutched a paisley shawl close
to her neck as she turned to cousin
Gerald. "Why is the doctor taking so
long?" she was pleading ...

The days of Claire's dream passed,
but the face of a strange Mama
remained worried and soon the sleeping
Claire was to learn why as the dream
began to return. In the new dream,

Voices and faces swam through her dreams

the sun was shining beyond the window drapes. Tears blurred its light as they blurred the needlepoint pictures on the wall. "I will ride! I will!" The vexation of it! The dream girl who was Elizabeth, or was it Claire, threw back the counterpane and dragged her legs around. Something stopped her going any further as, in disbelief, she lifted the cotton nightdress. One foot was perfect. The other, was missing from the end of her bandaged leg. A scream came from Claire's throat as she awoke and found herself sitting in her own dark bedroom, the covers thrown from her and sweat pouring down her neck and face.

"Claire! What is it?" Mrs. Sterston burst through the door rubbing sleep from her eyes.

Claire stared at her mother, then blinked. The alarm clock ticked its way past one o'clock on her bedside table. Teddy sat beside it and the light that came in from the landing was from an electric bulb. Claire leaned forward

and ran her hands down her legs deliberately feeling each of her toes. Slowly she shook her head. "A bad dream, that's all, Mum. I'm sorry I woke you." She lay back again, pulling the covers around her. It had seemed so real.

The next day was Christmas Eve and Red Hall was under a light covering of snow. Mrs. Sterston grumbled that she'd never get to the butcher in time and her chicken would be sold to someone else. To make the job easier, her husband went with her. Claire was left on her own at Red Hall to complete the job of arranging the Christmas cards above the mantelpiece.

When she ran out of drawing pins, she hopped her way through to the office and searched the old bureau her father had found in the attic and put to use as a desk. It was a lovely old thing, with inlaid marquetry birds on either side of the leather writing pad. Idly, Claire ran her fingers over them and jumped as she felt a spring click under one of the wooden beaks. The whole panel lifted easily on its hinges.

Inside was a sheaf of old photographs bound by a flimsy ribbon. The first five showed a young girl on a pony. She looked bold and carefree. The last one was different, not just because the horse was bigger or that the rider was older and wore a tailored, adult habit – the girl's expression had changed. She looked sad and determined. Claire sat down to examine the

For the Want of a Saddle

The whole panel lifted easily on its hinges

photograph more thoroughly. Her fingers tingled as she turned it to read the inscription on the back: "Elizabeth and Ginger, 1908."

A shiver ran over Claire's shoulders. Elizabeth ... the name was familiar, almost as if she had known the woman. Yet how could she! It was all so long ago. Elizabeth ... Claire spoke the name out loud and suddenly knew why this last photograph looked so odd – beneath the fixed pommel of the side saddle the girl's skirt hung empty.

The sound of footsteps in the passage startled Claire from her thoughts. "Mum ...?" Her voice trembled. Outside, Topper gave an uneasy neigh. A thief? Maybe they thought the house was empty ...

Grasping her stick, Claire hopped to the kitchen in time to see a dark figure in a long coat disappear into the stables. Without a second thought, Claire set out in pursuit.

Topper was moving in her box, ears pricked and eyes alert, but otherwise the stable was empty. Claire checked each of the stalls, then hauled herself up the ladder to the loft. Not a sign of anyone and all the windows were shut.

Had it been nothing more than her imagination?

A dark object in the corner caught Claire's attention. She heaved it down and found herself in possession of a side-saddle. It was old and dusty but the leather was still sound and it had been beautifully made.

The saddle badly needed cleaning,

but Topper next door was too close to resist. It took no time at all to slip a bridle on Topper and then the old saddle. It fitted as if it had been made for her. "What do you think of that?" Claire asked the chestnut mare. Topper flicked her ears and turned her head to look. Otherwise, she was remarkably unperturbed

There was a mounting block set in the stable wall. With a good deal of heaving, Claire reached the top step, then sat down and lifted her injured right leg carefully into place. The curved pommel fitted around it like a glove.

Her left foot sought out the stirrup and touched Topper's side as she took up the rein. The mare took one step then another, shifted herself under the weight then walked across the yard. Sitting tall, letting her body move naturally in time with the mare's, Claire felt so happy she could have burst into song.

Topper cocked an ear and turned to

the field, her head going up as she neighed loudly. Along the far hedge a girl rider came into view. Dark skirts flew behind her. For a moment she turned and as her eyes met Claire's she smiled. Then she was galloping down the hill and gathering her horse to jump the hedge and vanish ...

Claire rode Topper into the field beyond the hedge. The crisp snow was unmarked. A girl's laughter rang again but this time Claire knew it was only in her head. She smiled to herself and patted Topper's neck. Lisa had been right about Red Hall being haunted.

Would she ever see Elizabeth again, Claire wondered. She hoped so, because now she understood the meaning of her strange and troubled dreams. She had a lot to thank Elizabeth for. In fact, the best Christmas present she could have wished for was the chance she had been given to ride again by discovering that dusy old side-saddle.